Haiku

The 1988 Heideman Award-Winning One-Act Play

Katherine Snodgrass

A SAMUEL FRENCH ACTING EDITION

SAMUEL FRENCH

FOUNDED 1830

SAMUELFRENCH.COM
SAMUELFRENCH-LONDON.CO.UK

FOR PRODUCTION ENQUIRIES

UNITED STATES AND CANADA
Info@SamuelFrench.com
1-866-598-8449

UNITED KINGDOM AND EUROPE
Plays@SamuelFrench-London.co.uk
020-7255-4302

Each title is subject to availability from Samuel French, depending
upon country of performance. Please be aware that *HAIKU* may not be
licensed by Samuel French in your territory. Professional and amateur
producers should contact the nearest Samuel French office or licensing
partner to verify availability.

MUSIC USE NOTE

Licensees are solely responsible for obtaining formal written permission from copyright owners to use copyrighted music in the performance of this play and are strongly cautioned to do so. If no such permission is obtained by the licensee, then the licensee must use only original music that the licensee owns and controls. Licensees are solely responsible and liable for all music clearances and shall indemnify the copyright owners of the play(s) and their licensing agent, Samuel French, against any costs, expenses, losses and liabilities arising from the use of music by licensees. Please contact the appropriate music licensing authority in your territory for the rights to any incidental music.

IMPORTANT BILLING AND CREDIT REQUIREMENTS

If you have obtained performance rights to this title, please refer to your licensing agreement for important billing and credit requirements.

HAIKU was produced in workshop under the
auspices of The Philadelphia Theatre Company's
new play project STAGES (Lynn M. Thomson,
Program Director, Artistic Associate) on the
TUCC Stage III, Temple University City Center,
1619 Walnut Street, Philadelphia, PA, on April 26,
28 and 29, 1989, with the following cast and crew:

NELL .... Karen Higgins-Hurley
BILLIE.....................Maryann Plunkett
LOUISE........................ Alla Nedoresow

Director.................... Christopher Ashley
Set   Designer..........................Dan Boyles
Lighting Designer .... James Leitner
Music ....John Gromoda
Stage Manager...................Claudia Park

NOTES ON PRODUCTION

The draft that follows is the one closest to my original conception of the play. In acting it, character intentions should always come before any considerations of poetry.

It is my feeling that the play is weakest when the production tries to "answer" the questions that the script raises. The last moment in the play is meant to be ambiguous.

Kate Snodgrass

CHARACTERS

NELL   50's, Mother of Louise and Billie
LOUISE 20's-30's, Nell's youngest daughter
BILLIE   20's-30's, Nell's eldest daughter

TIME: Present

SETTING: A living room

NOTE: The set is suggestive rather than realistic. The flashback sequences may be signaled by light changes or sounds or both. A bamboo flute or porcelain wind chime may be substituted for the autoharp and/or used to signal the flashbacks, but the sound should remain delicate, almost eerie.

HAIKU

AT RISE: The stage is black. We hear an AUTOHARP. It goes from the top of the scale to the bottom. As LIGHTS come up, NELL has an obvious bruise on her wrist, a pad of paper and black magic marker in her lap, and a magnifying glass on a chain around her neck. LOUISE has a bandage on her forehead and is wearing a football helmet. The LIGHTING suggests a mystery.

NELL. You were born in early winter. John and I planned it that way. I couldn't imagine having a baby in the summertime. It gets so sticky in August, humid. A breach baby. You tried to back into the world. I remember, the doctor had to pull you out. It was night when they finally brought you to me.

LOUISE.

November evening.

Blackbirds scull across the moon.

My breath warms my hands.

NELL. *(She writes haiku, then checks it with the magnifying glass.)* John said you were too beautiful to live. It was true. You and Bebe together, you were like china dolls. Delicate,

7

perfect. And then...that day I saw you through the window. Billie was on the swing set, and you were there. Outside. She was in red, and you had on that blue jumpsuit, the corduroy one with the zipper. The ball lay beside you. And that momma doll that winked. You were so quiet. You'd stared before, of course, when something fascinated you, as all children do when they...as all children do. But this time, you were...different. I called for you to come inside. *Lulu, come inside and have some lunch!* But you didn't hear me. *Bebe, bring Lulu and come inside!* I went out then. I had to get down on my knees beside you. I touched your hair and then your face. I held up that momma doll, but you stared through it in a way that... Funny, I don't remember being afraid. I remember the look on your sister's face.

LOUISE.

Cold, chain-metal swings

Clang in the empty school yard.

Silent summer rain.

NELL. (*Writes haiku, same process as before.*) Do you know, I used to cry when school ended? It's true! I used to cry on the last day of school every year. My mother thought I was crazy. I'd come dragging my book bag over the fields, my face all wet. And my momma!

LOUISE. And my momma!

NELL. Nellie, she'd say...

LOUISE. Nellie, she'd say...you're the strangest girl I ever did see!

NELL. Yes, that's... What did you say?

LOUISE. That you're the strangest girl?

NELL. No, no. Before that. Are your tired?

LOUISE. Before that?

NELL. You are tired, and Billie's late.

LOUISE. Tell me again about John. Please. You haven't talked about John in a long time.

NELL. John. All right then. John was tall and thin like Icabod Crane, only not so scared.

LOUISE. John wasn't scared of anything.

NELL. He wasn't scared of anything, not John. He had a big, strong jaw and a tuft of yellow hair that stood up on his head, as yellow...

LOUISE. ...as Mr. Turner's daffodils.

NELL. At least. And he would take you on his knee. Do you remember the song he used to sing? *(NELL clears her throat and sings.) Here come a Lulu! Here come a Lulu to the Indian dance. (LOUISE joins in.) All of them Indians, all of them Indians dance around Lulu's tent. (Like a drum.) Here* come a Lulu! *Here* come Lulu! *Here* come a Lulu! *(They laugh, remembering.)*

LOUISE.
Icy branches bend
And break over stones. I hear
My dead father...laugh.

(NELL writes haiku, same process as before.)

LOUISE. Wasn't there a story about a fox? Who had a bushy tail?

NELL. You remember that?

LOUISE. And John would rub Bebe's back until she want to sleep. He smelled of soap and something...sweet?

NELL. (*Dryly.*) Sweet! Cigars from Havana.

LOUISE. (*Repeating with NELL'S exact inflection.*) Cigars from Havana.

NELL. We'll stop now. (*During this next exchange, NELL fishes in her pocket for a bottle of pills and takes a pill out.*)

LOUISE. No! No, I want to do more.

NELL. Louise—

LOUISE. I'm not ready to go back. Please, not now.

NELL. But Billie's not here yet. We've got to be careful.

LOUISE. But I can do it! I promise. Please, momma, I hate to go back. It's like being smothered!

NELL. I know.

LOUISE. Everything is so dim, and I can't hear you properly. Or see you or touch you or...(*Seeing the bruise on NELL's wrist—*) Did I do that?

NELL. It's not bad.

LOUISE. That was before I knew what to do. Please. I can stop it now, I know I can. You said so yourself.

NELL. I know what I said.

LOUISE. If you don't let me try, I'll never learn what to do.

NELL. We can talk to Bebe tomorrow. Today, it would be better—

LOUISE. Today, it would be better—if I saw Bebe first. Then I can stand it.

(During this next exchange NELL tries to give LOUISE a pill. LOUISE refuses. NELL removes the helmet.)

NELL. No. Not today!

LOUISE. Not today!

NELL. You're too tired.

LOUISE. I can control it.

NELL. Louise. I don't want to wait too long. You'll hurt yourself.

LOUISE. You'll hurt yourself. I mean, no! I won't. You promised I could talk to Bebe. You said I *had* to talk to her.

NELL. Yes, yes, we will. Tomorrow. *(NELL holds out pill.)* I want you to take this now.

LOUISE. *(Stubborn.)* You promised I could wait for Bebe.

NELL. I want you to—

LOUISE. I need some water. *(NELL is silent.)* I do! I can't swallow.

NELL. Louise.

LOUISE. I can't swallow. My throat is dry.

NELL. *(Sighing.)* Yes, all right, just a minute. *(NELL exits.)*

LOUISE. Just a minute. Just a minute.

(A loud door SLAM startles LOUISE. Abruptly, LIGHTS come full up as BILLIE enters with a suitcase and packages. There is a moment of recognition between LOUISE and BILLIE. LOUISE might say BILLIE's name, but NELL enters with a glass of water. There is an awkwardness in this next exchange. NELL greets BILLIE and moves to LOUISE with the pill.)

BILLIE. Nell, how are you? You look exhausted. I thought I'd never make it. The traffic at the airport is worse than ever.

NELL. You're here.

BILLIE. Yes, I'm here.

NELL. You're late.

BILLIE. I'm sorry. Are you all right? You sounded so strange on the telephone.

NELL. I? Yes. *(Pause. LOUISE refuses to take the pill.)*

BILLIE. *(Half-kidding.)* Shall I leave again come back?

NELL. No. No, of course not. We don't mind at all, do we, Lulu? *(Holding up pill, asking.)* Can you *tell* Bebe how we don't mind?

LOUISE. *(To BILLIE.)* We don't mind.

NELL. *(Putting pill away.)* Michael's not with you?

BILLIE. No. No, he's not coming. *(Then quickly to...)* Look what I came across in a little shop in Boston. They had both of your books, is that unbelievable? And get this, they actually had them in the poetry section. I get so tired of searching through the books on Japanese culture. Do you need them, or can I keep them? You know, I really love the cover on this last one.

NELL. Oh, Billie, I wish you'd waited. I was going to send you a copy, but...

BILLIE. They're finally getting the hang of it at that place. Black and white photography is much closer to what you wanted all along, isn't it?

NELL. I've been so busy. I don't know how I could have forgotten to send you...

BILLIE. Of course, I had to see that lovely dedication. I'm such a push-over. It always gives me a little thrill to see my name in print even if it *is* after the fact.

NELL. Let me go upstairs and—

BILLIE. I was just so surprised to run across them, and I was really impressed with this new cover. Where did they find the photographer?

NELL. I'll give you your copy now.

BILLIE. No, mother, mother, really! This one's fine. Well, it's not as if I can't afford it. At least it's not one of those dry biographies you used to write, the lives of the saints or some such thing? Somehow with you I always feel like a groupie at the stage door. "Please, ma'am, it's a first edition and would you sign it, please?"

NELL. I've already signed your copy. But if you want me to sign this, too...Why don't I do it later, all right? Let me do it later when Lulu's asleep. That way, we—

BILLIE. Fine, sure. Later is fine, whatever. Oh, I brought something for Lulu, too. (*BILLIE brings out package from her large bag and holds it out to NELL. It is wrapped in very shiny wrapping paper with a bright ribbon.*)

NELL. You did? Why, that was thoughtful. What is it?

LOUISE. What is it?

BILLIE. Open it. Oh hell, it's another music box.

LOUISE. Oh hell.

NELL. It's wrapped so prettily, why don't you let Lulu open it?

BILLIE. Do we have time before Easter?

NELL. Billie.

BILLIE. I'm sorry. Really. But she won't care what's inside. She just likes the wrapping paper.

NELL. That's not true. Lulu loves music.

LOUISE. Lulu loves music.

BILLIE. Lulu loves wrapping paper.

NELL. (*To BILLIE.*) Go on. You give it to her.

(*Flashback sequence begins. They are children. Dolls are mimed.*)

BILLIE. I have to give this to you. This is the baby doll, and this is the momma doll. Now you take the baby doll and rock her to sleep, like this. (*Singing.*) *Rocka-bye baby in the treetop. When* *the wind blows...*That's right. You be the babysitter. And now the momma comes to play with the baby. Hello, baby.

LOUISE. Hello, baby.

BILLIE. My, you are sleeping so soundly I don't want to wake you up. How did my baby do today, Mrs. Lippoman? Was she a good baby?

LOUISE. Was she a good baby?

BILLIE. Let me see her. Isn't she the most beautiful baby in the whole—No, give it back. No you can't have the momma doll. You have the baby doll.

LOUISE. You have the baby doll.

BILLIE. No, let go.

LOUISE. No.

BILLIE. Give it back, you can't have both of them.

LOUISE. Both of them.

BILLIE. (*New tactic.*) All right then, give me the baby doll.

LOUISE. Give me the baby doll.

BILLIE. Give it to me. It's my momma doll, and it's my baby doll. Let go, let go...!

LOUISE. Let go,let go! (*Baby doll breaks.*)

BILLIE. You broke it! That was my baby doll. It was mine, and I'm going to tell on you, you...

LOUISE. You...

BILLIE. I didn't want to play with you anyway. You're stupid, stupid!

LOUISE. Stupid!

BILLIE. I'm going to tell, and then I'll never have to play with you again. Not ever! (*BILLIE shoves LOUISE's forehead with the palm of her hand.*)

LOUISE. Not ever! (*LOUISE begins hitting herself in the forehead.*)

BILLIE. Stop hurting yourself!

(*Flashback sequence ends.*)

BILLIE. Is she hurting herself again? What's that bandage for?

NELL. No, no, of course not. We just had a little accident.

BILLIE. Isn't the medicine working?

NELL. Of course, yes.

BILLIE. Let's look at it.

NELL. No, it's perfectly fine now. Almost healed.

BILLIE. Did you get that bruise at the same time?

NELL. Oh, this? It's nothing. I don't even remember where I got it.

LOUISE. (*Holds up her hands for a hug.*) Bebe.

BILLIE. Good lord. (*LOUISE and BILLIE hug.*)

NELL. That's new, isn't it?

BILLIE. What?

NELL. She's different than when you saw her last, isn't she?

BILLIE. Because she hugged me? We all know how much that means.

NELL. Billie, what will we do with you?

BILLIE. Well, they're supposed to get more affectionate as they get older. I might as well be a rag doll that she's fond of. But if that's what you mean, that she's more responsive, then yes, we can thank whatever gods there be that she's not gone the other way. At least the medicine is doing that for her.

NELL. The medicine.

BILLIE. Yes.

NELL. But don't you think she's getting better, though? Honestly, isn't she more alert?

BILLIE. Alert.

NELL. She knew you, Billie. She wanted to touch you.

BILLIE. Of course she knows me. I'm her sister. She's wanted to get her hands around my neck for years.

LOUISE. For years.

BILLIE. (*Laughing.*) There, you see? All right, all right, let's try this. (*She takes wrapped present and holds it out to LOUISE.*) Ah, it's a lovely bow, isn't it? And look at that shiny wrapping paper. You love that, don't you? Look at her. I tell you, Nell, I wasted my money on the music box. This wrapping paper's going to be enough.

NELL. Let's just take this bow off. Here.

BILLIE. No fair, no fair helping.

NELL. Now this paper comes off.

(*LOUISE tears the paper off the music box. She opens the box as it tinkles out a song. She is enthralled.*)

NELL. There, now. There. Why, that's beautiful, isn't it, Lulu? That's beautiful. See, see how she loves the music?

BILLIE. Yes.

NELL. Look, look at her. And she unwrapped it herself.

BILLIE. Mother.

NELL. She knew exactly—

BILLIE. No.

NELL. —what to do. Don't you see a difference in her?

BILLIE. (*During this speech, BILLIE takes the box, handing the shiny paper back to LOUISE.*) You never change, do you? No, I don't see any difference. She's not more alert, and she's not getting any better. All right. All right, maybe she's a little more affectionate. Maybe. But that's natural. Most of them become more affectionate. They learn to feed themselves and to go to the bathroom and to hug their sisters when they come home to visit.

NELL. (*Taking shiny paper from LOUISE.*) You don't understand. You can't possibly know, you don't see her every day.

BILLIE. Yes, and you do, and you take every gaze out the window and rationalize it into some sort of normal reaction.

NELL. I don't rationalize. I don't need to. I see real change for the better!

BILLIE. Better, momma?

(Second flashback sequence. Again, they are children.)

BILLIE. Better bring her inside, momma. She's staring at the sun again. Maa-maa! *(There is no answer, so BILLIE uses a shiny necklace (or a prism) from around her own neck and holds it up for LOUISE who is captivated with the shine. Singing.) Twinkle, twinkle, little star, how I wonder who you are.* Oooo, pretty twinkle, pretty twinkle. Maa-maa! *(She sings a song to the tune of "Frere Jacques". LOUISE hums some notes.)*

Where is Lulu? Where is Lulu?
Here I am, here I am.
How are you this morning?
Very well, I thank you
(BILLIE pulls LOUISE to her feet.)
Please stand up. Please sit down.
(BILLIE pulls LOUISE back down.)
Where is Booboo? Where is Booboo?
(Pointedly.)
Here you are, here you are.
How are you this morning?
Very well, I thank you.

(BILLIE pulls LOUISE to her feet.)
Please stand up. Please sit down.
(BILLIE pulls LOUISE back down. She begins
to substitute different sounds for LOUISE's name.
LOUISE imitates, repeating only the last sounds.)
Where is Poopoo? Where is—
LOUISE. —Poopoo. *(Pause.)*
BILLIE.
Where is...Bongbong?
LOUISE. Bongbong.

(BILLIE gives up on the song and does the sounds
rhythmically and playfully as LOUISE
follows, repeating each set of sounds. BILLIE
begins enjoying LOUISE, who mirrors even
facial expressions. [Different sounds may be
repeated or substituted as the actors play.])

BILLIE. *(and LOUISE after. Grunting.)*
Ugghh-Ugghhh. (Tongue out.) Blah-blah. Eeeek-
eeeek. *(Like a villain.)* Heh-heh-heh. *(Rolling*
the tongue.) Thrrrrrthrrrr. *(Like a pig.)* Snort-
snort. Snort-snort. Snort-snort. *(As the sounds*
become funny to her, BILLIE laughs. LOUISE
laughs. BILLIE laughs again. LOUISE imitates.
When she realizes that LOUISE is not playing
with her but only repeating, BILLIE holds up the
chain/prism again.)
BILLIE. Pretty twinkle, pretty twinkle. I
wish... *(End of flashback sequence.)* I wish I
could understand you, momma.

NELL. I know you've never been able to understand. You were too young, I suppose. It was asking too much of you.

BILLIE. Was it? Strange. I don't remember being asked. Is that why you don't dedicate your books to Lulu?

NELL. What?

BILLIE. Yes, is that your way of asking me to understand now?

NELL. No, Bebe, I never—

BILLIE. Why not to Lulu? Because she can't *ever* understand?

NELL. No, that's not it at all. We've been wanting to talk to you. That's why I telephoned.

BILLIE. Because of the dedication?

NELL. Yes, and...and—

BILLIE. I thought it was because of your eyes.

NELL. Well, yes. That too.

BILLIE. How much can you see, anyway?

NELL. I can make out your shape, but it's getting worse.

LOUISE. It's getting worse. (*Silence.*)

BILLIE. All right,then. Will Daddy's trust fund cover a nurse for Lulu?

NELL. Even if it would, I don't want some stranger in the house caring for Lulu. I'll do it myself.

BILLIE. Yourself? Mother, how?

NELL. I'll manage. I've done it up until now.

BILLIE. But what if she dirties her clothes? What if she has a reaction? What if you were to fall? Lulu couldn't help you. She wouldn't know what to do. Why, she wouldn't even understand that anything was wrong.

NELL. I do not have to have help.

BILLIE. Then why did you ask me—?

NELL. I've managed this long, and besides...

BILLIE. Yes?

NELL. Lulu understands more than you know.

LOUISE. More than you know.

BILLIE. Lulu understands what *you want* her to understand. Momma, you can't go on ignoring Lulu's illness.

NELL. I'm not ignoring—

BILLIE. Mother, listen to me. Put her in a hospital where she can be taken care of properly. No, wait, I can help you. Please. Michael and I have talked it over, and...Really. I'd be happy if you'd come live with us. I thought that's what you wanted. You can visit Lulu every day if you want to. You can sit with her. Please. It's not as if she's going to know where she is.

NELL. Of course she knows where she is! What are you talking about? You haven't heard what I've been trying to say.

BILLIE. What haven't I heard?

NELL. That she's different.She's changed.

BILLIE. Changed how? And if you say she's more affectionate—

NELL. It's not just that. It's more. Much more. I haven't told you before this because I knew you wouldn't believe me. But you don't live with her, Billie, you don't see. You asked why I dedicate the haiku to you and never to Louise. It's because ... I don't write the haiku.

BILLIE. What?

NELL. It's Louise.

LOUISE. It's Louise. (*Silence.*)

BILLIE. No.

NELL. It's true.

BILLIE. That's impossible.

NELL. No, I swear it.

LOUISE. I swear it.

BILLIE. Momma.

NELL. It started three years ago after we changed to that new medication.

BILLIE. What started?

NELL. I was reading a book. Very absorbed. Lulu was sitting, as she always does, next to the window. Suddenly I realized that I had forgotten to give her the afternoon pill. I glanced up, and she was sitting forward in her chair, leaning on the sill.(*LOUISE does this as NELL speaks.*) It was odd. I knew she wouldn't notice me, but I said her name, *Lulu?* And she turned to me and looked at me, *really looked at me,* for the first time. She asked me to forgive her. Hah! As if there was anything to forgive. She was so frightened, so frightened. Bebe, it's as if she's trapped, trapped in a maze, and everything's all white, like cotton, or clouds, and...and she can't get out. Everything moves so slowly. And when she trys, sounds come in to distract her. They pull her away, and she can't concentrate. She can't be herself. But she was there. She is. *Louise* is there.

LOUISE. Can't concentrate.

BILLIE. You mean she's...normal...without the medication, or—?

NELL. No, it's not that. She still—Well, she can't go on without the medicine. I have to give her the medicine. She needs it.

BILLIE. Then what—?

NELL. Because it was late! The medicine has to be late. I don't understand it. I don't pretend to.

BILLIE. Wait. Are you saying that now you deliberately hold back her medicine?

NELL. Yes, yes! She can't get out without my help!

BILLIE. Dear God.

NELL. I used to think I was making it up.

BILLIE. I can imagine.

NELL. But I'm not. I'm not. The haiku is real. Louise is real.

BILLIE. Why didn't you tell me this before?

NELL. I didn't dare believe it myself. Then when we started working, we decided it was better if no one knew for the time being.

BILLIE. Why?

NELL. It was so fragile, don't you see? So delicate. It doesn't happen all the time. Sometimes when her medicine is late. But even then, not every day. And she only stays for a little before we have to take the medicine.

BILLIE. I see. And she speaks...in poetry.

NELL. No, no. We were at the window. It was October and just about dusk. Mr. Turner was burning leaves in his incinerator out back. I said, "Look how beautiful the colors are. Late autumn." And she said, "Late autumn evening/Swallows circle overhead/Wood smoke curling up." By concentrating on what we could see through the window, we'd make a haiku together. After that, she began making them up on her own. I simply sit and talk, and...Billie, it's as if she sees my thoughts, my innermost feelings, and translates them into images.

BILLIE. Almost as if she were you.

NELL. Yes.

BILLIE. What do you talk about?

NELL. Nothing important. Memories. The past. But she'll take the most ordinary event and make it so personal somehow.

BILLIE. Yes. How long do you talk?

NELL. Not long.

BILLIE. *How* long?

NELL. Half an hour at the most. But she's trying very hard. She wants to practice. She wants to be...

BILLIE. You want her to be normal.

NELL. No. More than that. Extraordinary. And she is.

BILLIE. Mother, if this is true...I mean, *when* this happens...Why haven't you told the doctors?

NELL. No doctors and no more hospitals. They brought on this problem in the first place. If I hadn't rushed her to the doctors so quickly, maybe she would have come out of it. No! We don't know! If they didn't have her taking all these drugs...Nobody knows what might have happened!

LOUISE. Nobody knows.

BILLIE. All right, if you mean that, then take her off the drugs entirely.

NELL. We can't do that.

BILLIE. Why not?

NELL. She hurts herself! She could—!

BILLIE. Momma, if that's what you believe, take her off the drugs. We could put her in the hospital and have the drug levels monitored.

NELL. No. I told you no hospitals.

BILLIE. But they could even wean her off the drugs slowly, and then we could—

NELL. No!

BILLIE. *Why not?*

LOUISE. *Why not?*

NELL. She needs the drugs. She's not herself yet. She needs them to...to protect her until...It's a question of will power.

BILLIE. Whose, yours?

NELL. I knew you wouldn't understand. I warned her, but no! She said she wanted to let you in. She said we *had* to tell you.

BILLIE. *She* said that?

NELL. She loves you, Bebe. The way she hugged you today was only a tiny indication of that.

BILLIE. Why did you ask me here?

NELL. I can barely see to write the words anymore. Don't you understand?

BILLIE. I'm sorry.

NELL. I need your help, Bebe. We need you.

(Flashback sequence. BILLIE is teaching LOUISE about make-up. The lipstick, mirror, etc., is mimed. BILLIE pushes hair back from LOUISE's forehead.)

BILLIE. *(To LOUISE.)* You need to keep your hair out of your face. Okay, now, you take the lipstick and you put it on like...that. See? Okay. Pucker up. *(BILLIE puckers, and LOUISE imitates her as BILLIE applies lipstick to LOUISE's mouth, then to her own.)* Mmmm, luscious pink!

LOUISE. Mmmm.

BILLIE. Now then, you take this pencil. And *don't* put it in your eye!

LOUISE. *Don't* put it in your eye!

BILLIE. *(To mirror.)* You draw around the eye...underneath...above...but not too much. There. See?

LOUISE. *Don't* put it in your eye!

BILLIE. Right. And now for the shadow. What color shall we use? Let's use turquoise or...What about this purple? Yeah, let's use the purple!

LOUISE. Yeah, let's use the purple!

(*BILLIE puts it on for the mirror while LOUISE picks up the turquoise and draws big circles over her neck, her face, her cheeks and forehead.*)

BILLIE. And we put it above the crease of the eye, not just on the lid. Then we take this black pencil and we draw it out, just like Elizabeth Taylor did in *Cleopatra*. Now, then, what's next?

LOUISE. Now, then, what's next? (*BILLIE looks at LOUISE and reacts as NELL enters.*)

BILLIE. Oh...!

NELL. Billie, how could you!

LOUISE. How could you!

NELL. (*Begins wiping off the makeup.*) I thought you knew better than this. What were you thinking of? Oh, Lulu, such a mess.

LOUISE. Mess!

NELL. Her face is as red as a fire engine. And this turquoise! It'll take days for these colors to wear off. Why on earth...?

(*LOUISE begins slapping her legs.*)

NELL. Now you've done it! Here, hold her hands. This is not the first time this has happened, but by God it will be the last. For the final time, do not take it upon yourself to teach her. You leave that to me, or you can leave this house! Do you understand? (*BILLIE lets go of LOUISE's hands.*) Oh, now I've got it all over me. Lulu, *be still!* (*Surprisingly, LOUISE is still.*) Bebe. (*End of flashback sequence.*)

NELL. Bebe.

BILLIE. What do you want me to do?

NELL. I want for you, I *need* for you to listen to her and believe in her so that she can be who she is. If we believe, she can get well. We can help her, I know it. Let us show you. Louise? Louise, Billie's here.

BILLIE. She's not listening.

NELL. Billie's here, and you wanted to talk to her. Remember? (*LOUISE looks at BILLIE.*) You see? There. Now, Bebe, say something to her. Go on.

BILLIE. Mother, don't make me do this.

NELL. Lulu. It's Billie.

LOUISE. Bebe.

BILLIE. Lulu.

NELL. Ask her something.

BILLIE. Mother.

NELL. Ask her.

BILLIE. All right. Lulu. Is it really you?

LOUISE. Is it really you?

BILLIE. Yes, it's really me. Is it true?

LOUISE. True?

BILLIE. (*Looks back at NELL for encouragement. NELL is insistent.*) It's been a

long time since I've seen you, Lulu. It's been
months and months, I think. How...How are you?

LOUISE. How are you?

BILLIE. I've been fine, but how are you?
(*Pause*.)

LOUISE. I've been fine.

BILLIE. She's just repeating, Mother.

NELL. She's tired. We were writing just
before you got here. It's hard, but she can do it.
Concentrate, Lulu. This is important. It's Billie.
(*To BILLIE*.) Ask her about the poems.

BILLIE. Yes, I've read the poems. They're
lovely.

LOUISE. We were writing just before you got
here.

NELL. You see?

BILLIE. Momma told me. I want so much to
believe it's true.

LOUISE. Believe it's true.

BILLIE. No, no, say something else. Say
anything else. Make up a poem. Can you do that
for me? Make up a poem. Please do that.

LOUISE. Make up a poem?

BILLIE. Yes, yes, please.

NELL. Look out the window. Describe it to
her.

BILLIE. (*To LOUISE*.) Look, look out there.
Winter's nearly over. Mr. Turner's daffodils
are in bloom. And the hydrangea bushes we
planted that year daddy died. Remember?
They're big now. Why, they cover the whole side

of the porch. Momma's already put out that old
bird feed—I can't do this.

NELL. Keep going, she's listening.

BILLIE. She's not. You are, momma.

NELL. Please.

BILLIE. Well then...(*To the window.*) It's
almost sunset. The sky is...red.

'NELL. Yes. Red sky at dusk.

LOUISE. Red sky at dusk.

BILLIE. One gray cloud...lies just...over the
trees...

LOUISE. Over the trees...one gray cloud lies—

BILLIE. She's mimicking me.

LOUISE. —in my sister...

BILLIE. (*Comforting.*) That's right, I am
your sister, aren't I?

LOUISE. (*Grabbing BILLIE's hand.*) —in
my sister's...sister's—

NELL. In my —

LOUISE. (*Gesturing.*) —sister's—

NELL. (*Prompting.*) —sister's...

BILLIE. Mother.

NELL. (*Understanding.*) ...eyes!

LOUISE. —eyes!

NELL. There. (*NELL claps.*) Bravo, Lulu!
Good girl!

BILLIE. Stop it!

NELL. What.

BILLIE. She's repeating.

NELL. No.

LOUISE. No.

BILLIE. She's repeating what I say and what you say.

NELL. No, no! Louise, help me now.

BILLIE. Don't put us through this.

NELL. Louise?

BILLIE. I can't bear it.

LOUISE. I can't bear it.

NELL. Try a little harder, baby.

BILLIE. Mother, listen to me!

NELL. Concentrate now.

BILLIE. Please, don't!

LOUISE. Listen to me!

BILLIE. Mother, you have got to—

NELL. Louise, look at me and—

BILLIE. *Mother, stop!*

(*LOUISE is startled by the shout and begins screaming and banging her head. Both NELL and BILLIE shout over the screaming. BILLIE gets the football helmet but can't get it onto LOUISE.*)

NELL. The helmet. Lulu, Lulu, there.

BILLIE. Where is her medicine?

NELL. Oh, my hand! Hold her arms! (*Instead, BILLIE gets the music box and opens it for LOUISE to see. LOUISE immediately calms and focuses on the MUSIC. NELL gives LOUISE the pill and some water. BILLIE and NELL recover.*)

BILLIE. Will she be all right now?

NELL. Yes. If we can keep her quiet, the pill should take hold. We startled her.

BILLIE. How can you do this?

NELL. I hate to see her leave. I know what you're going to say. But every word I've told you is true. You didn't want to believe.

BILLIE. That's not true. I want to believe. Just don't ask me to see something that isn't there.

NELL. Then let us prove it to you. We'll try again tomorrow.

BILLIE. No, no. I don't want to try anymore. I've tried before. I can't keep trying and have it not be true.

NELL. It doesn't always happen, so I'm not promising anything.

BILLIE. No.

NELL. Bebe.

BILLIE. No, it hurts too much. You talk to her as if...

NELL. ...as if she's real. As if she's there. And she is.

BILLIE. Yes. Yes.

NELL. She is. Let me try tomor—

BILLIE. No.

NELL. I'm not asking you to believe it.

BILLIE. Aren't you?

NELL. I'm only asking you to let me try. Wait and see.

BILLIE. Wait and see.

NELL. You'll do that, won't you? Just that? For me?

*(Silence. LOUISE has closed the MUSIC BOX.
LIGHTS slowly begin fading back to the
setting with which we began the play.)*

BILLIE. For you? Yes.

NELL. You'll wait.

BILLIE. I think I can do that.

NELL. That's my Bebe. You can stay as long
as you like, you know. As long as you need to.
(Silence.)

BILLIE. It's spring.

NELL. Yes. Finally. Did I ever tell you—
when I was a girl, we had a cherry tree in the
backyard. It was just big enough for me to sit in.
The thickest branch was my backrest. It was
curved, like a hammock, and I could lean back
into that tree and rest my legs on either side of the
trunk. In the spring and summer, I took books out
there and devoured them along with the cherries.
The Brontes, Alexander Dumas. Jane Austen and
I were surrounded by flowers. The perfume.

BILLIE. I was never very literary. I can't
even make a good rhyme.

NELL. You're your father all over again.

BILLIE. He wasn't scared of anything, not
John. But I am, momma.

NELL. No, John wasn't scared of anything.

BILLIE. I wish daddy could be here to...see his
garden. *(Silence. BILLIE and NELL are together.*

They do not attend LOUISE, who is alone at the
window, separate.)
    LOUISE.
    Walking in his garden,
    Suddenly in the twilight—
    White hydrangea.

(Fade to...)

BLACKOUT

Furniture and Property List

On stage:
Oriental rug; Wicker armchair; Side table;
High-backed wooden chair; Wooden stool or
wicker ottoman; Two-dimensional tree,
branching in arc over rug; Window frame,
hanging up stage center.

Personal: NELL-- Magnifying glass on
chain; Pad of paper; Hair brush (optional); Black
magic marker or dark pen; Bottle containing
pills.

LOUISE--Football helmet, bandage
on forehead.

Off stage:

Personal: NELL--Glass of water

BILLIE: 2 volumes of poetry (one with
black and white cover); Shiny neck chain or
prism (worn on entrance); Music box wrapped in
shiny paper with a ribbon; Suitcase; Large tote
bag.

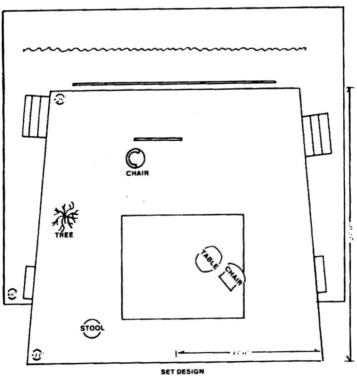

SET DESIGN
"HAIKU"